LUCKY

This book is dedicated to Our Lady, Star of the Sea—
guide and protectress of seafarers.

And to my husband, Marc, and my children, Owen, Oliver, Eila, &
Barrett, who make me feel like the luckiest wife and mom.

Lucky
Copyright © 2022 by Christy Mandin
All rights reserved. Manufactured in Italy.
No part of this book may be used or reproduced in any manner whatsoever without written permission
except in the case of brief quotations embodied in critical articles and reviews. For information address
HarperCollins Children's Books, a division of HarperCollins Publishers, 195 Broadway, New York, NY 10007.

www.harpercollinschildrens.com

Library of Congress Control Number: 2021933223
ISBN 978-0-06-304734-1

The artist used Procreate to create the digital illustrations for this book.
Typography by Christy Mandin and Chelsea C. Donaldson

22 23 24 25 26 RTLO 10 9 8 7 6 5 4 3 2 1
❖
First Edition

LUCKY

CHRISTY MANDIN

WITHDRAWN

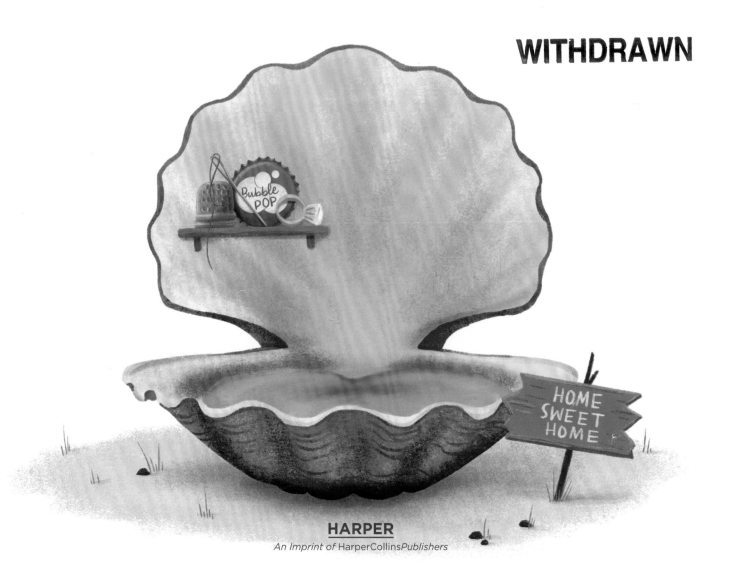

HARPER
An Imprint of HarperCollinsPublishers

Under a sparkling sea . . .

. . . lived a little pearl named Lucky.

WHAM!

Oh jeez Louise.

Bubble POP

Lucky had grown used to things falling from the sky.
It seemed like every day something new tumbled down
and nestled itself in the sand.

But Lucky could remember a long time ago when things had first begun to fall. They were shiny and small and quite interesting.

She'd felt like the luckiest little pearl in the deep blue sea.

She had the nicest shell, a beautiful view,
and plenty of knickknacks, too.

The one thing Lucky didn't have
was someone to share them with.

But she got along
just fine all by herself.

I am my own
best friend.

Then one day, something bizarre came crashing down from the sky. Heading straight toward her beautiful shell!

OLD
RUSTY
GARBAGE
BARGE

Lucky was sad, but she was a pearl
of great determination. She knew just
what she had to do.

She'd find a new home, complete with a gorgeous view and plenty of space for new knickknacks.
     Someplace safer and quieter, where maybe things wouldn't fall on her so much.

Things got off to a bumpy start.

Lucky tried this thing

and that thing

and one of these, too.

She even tried wearing a home like a crab. But it was trickier than it looked.

Lucky was beginning to worry her luck had run out when something new landed with a *thud* right on her head. It didn't hurt, though. In fact, it was rather squishy!

Hi! I'm Jelly the Jimfish.

Jim knew a thing or two about unluckiness.
He was a nice enough fellow, but no one
wanted a high five from a jellyfish.

Or a hug.

Plus he was a bit clumsy

and quite the chatterbox.

Jim wished for just enough luck to find a friend.

But Lucky didn't have time to be that for Jim. She was on a mission. She told him *all* about her plan to find a new home.

You're welcome to tag along with me. But I must stay focused and stick to the plan. Finding a home is the most important thing on my list.

THE DROP-OFF

CRAB COVE

ANEMONE ALLEY

As the two set out, Jim talked and talked (and talked some more) about everything and anything on his mind. And there was a lot on his mind.

Lucky grew more and more
impatient with him, until finally . . .

Lucky liked Jim, but he was too distracting.

She scurried off before
he could say another word.

Lucky continued her search, walking and walking until her little legs couldn't walk anymore. She was worried she would never find the right home. Just as she was about to give up, Lucky rounded a patch of coral and spotted the perfect shell in the most perfect spot, exactly like her old one!

She got straight to work settling in.
But something wasn't right.

Her shiny new home didn't
make her feel like the luckiest pearl.

Lucky headed out once more
to find the missing pieces.

As she neared a kelp forest, she heard some all-too-familiar sounds.

She cautiously peeked around
the leaves and found . . .

FIN

FISH FACTS ABOUT OCEAN POLLUTION

Did you see some things in Lucky and Jim's ocean home that don't belong? Each year billions of pounds of trash from human activities end up in the ocean. Lucky and Jim made the best of this unfortunate situation, but other sea creatures and marine life can't do that. They're forced to live under floating garbage patches and marine debris that pose a threat to their safety and survival.

Did you know plastic can take up to four hundred years to decompose? Some single-use plastics are meant to be used once and tossed in the trash right after! Drinking straws, plastic forks, and water bottles are some examples.

Scientists think jellyfish could help fight the problem of plastic pollution. Their slime traps tiny bits of plastic and might be useful in water filters or at factories that produce microplastics. Jim could be a real help in the fight to save our oceans! But he can't do it on his own. He needs our help.

WHAT you CAN DO...

STOP BUYING PLASTIC WATER BOTTLES.

Use a stainless steel or glass reusable bottle. These are infinitely recyclable.

BRING WHAT YOU NEED WITH YOU—INCLUDING YOUR LUNCH.

Pack a reusable straw, fork, knife, and spoon. Keep a clean set in your bag so you are always ready to eat on the go.

AVOID PRODUCTS THAT CONTAIN MICROBEADS.

We find these tiny plastic particles in face scrubs, toothpastes, and body washes. They enter our oceans and waterways through our sewer systems. These microplastics are labeled "polyethylene" and "polypropylene" in the ingredients label of your products.

PURCHASE FOODS IN BULK AND AVOID UNNECESSARILY PACKAGED FOOD ITEMS,

such as produce wrapped in plastic. Beeswax wraps can replace some plastic sandwich bags and plastic wrap.

ORGANIZE A BEACH CLEANUP.

Bring your friends and family to the beach and spend the day collecting plastic, trash, and marine debris.

LEARN FROM ORGANIZATIONS DEDICATED TO PROTECTING OUR OCEANS:

The Plastic Soup Foundation
Oceanic Society
Plastic Pollution Coalition
5 Gyres

Now that you know more about ocean pollution, see how many things you can find in this book that don't belong in our oceans.